MARC BROWN

ARTHUR'S UNDERWEAR

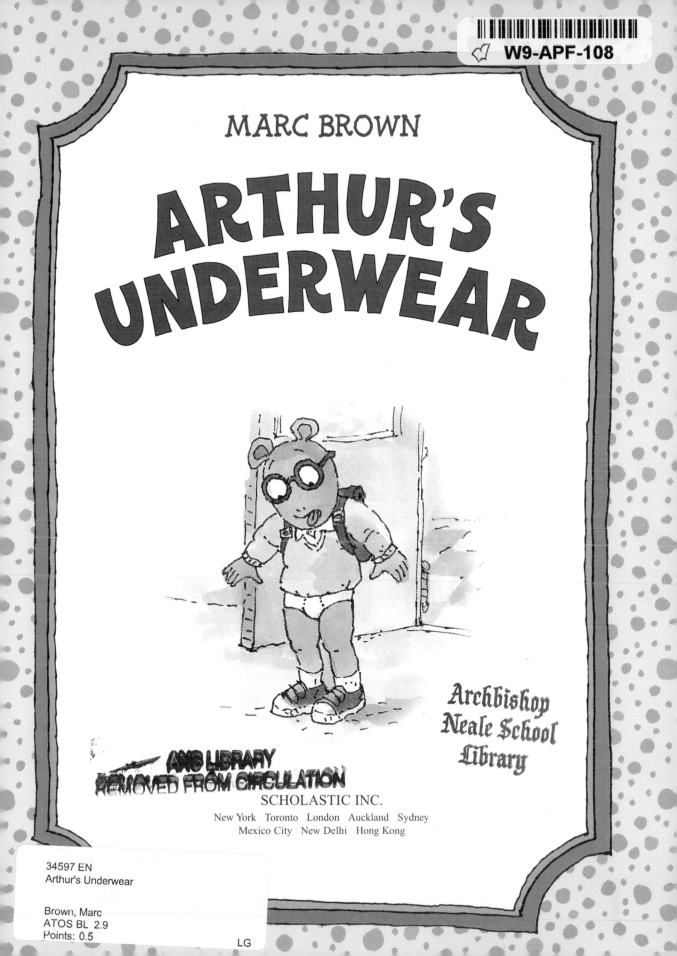

Archbishop
Neale School
Library

SCHOLASTIC INC.

New York   Toronto   London   Auckland   Sydney
Mexico City   New Delhi   Hong Kong

For all the kids
who insisted on an
underwear book

ISBN 0-439-20210-8

Copyright © 1999 by Marc Brown. All rights reserved. Published by
Scholastic Inc., 555 Broadway, New York, NY 10012,
by arrangement with Little, Brown and Company (Inc.).
Arthur® is a registered trademark of Marc Brown.
SCHOLASTIC and associated logos are trademarks
and/or registered trademarks of Scholastic Inc.

12 11 10 9 8 7 6 5 4 3   1 2 3 4 5/0

Printed in the U.S.A.   24

First Scholastic printing, September 2000

Binky Barnes was at the board doing a difficult problem.
"That's correct," said Mr. Ratburn. "Very good."

Binky cheered, "Yes!" and dropped his chalk. As he bent
down, the class heard a loud *RRRIPPP!*
Everyone laughed, except Mr. Ratburn. "Go to the office
and ask Ms. Tingley to sew them up," he said.

That afternoon at softball practice, when Binky
came up to bat, Arthur thought about Binky in his
underwear and laughed.
During dinner, Mom asked, "Anything interesting
happen at school today?"
Arthur started to laugh.
"What's so funny?" asked D.W.
But Arthur couldn't stop laughing to answer.

The next morning, Arthur woke up late.
He hurried through breakfast and ran most of the way
to school.
"Sorry I'm late, Mr. Ratburn! I guess my alarm —"
Everyone burst out laughing.
"Mr. Read, being late is one thing," said Mr. Ratburn,
"but not wearing any trousers — *that* is quite another!"
Arthur looked down — and screamed!

Arthur's scream woke him up.
Wow, he thought, *what a horrible dream!*

In school, the class watched a science film. "The amoeba is a single-celled life form. . . ."
Arthur's eyelids began to droop.

Suddenly, an amoeba that looked a lot like Arthur appeared on the screen. Its pants fell down, showing its underwear.

"Help!" cried Arthur-Amoeba. "I need my pants!"
All the other amoebas started to laugh.

Arthur-Amoeba was too embarrassed to move. Then
he felt someone shaking him.
"Wake up, Arthur!" said Buster. "The movie's over."

At lunch, Arthur didn't feel like eating.
"What should I do, Buster? Every time I go to sleep, I'm in my underwear!"
"Try staying awake," Buster suggested. "You can't dream if you don't sleep."

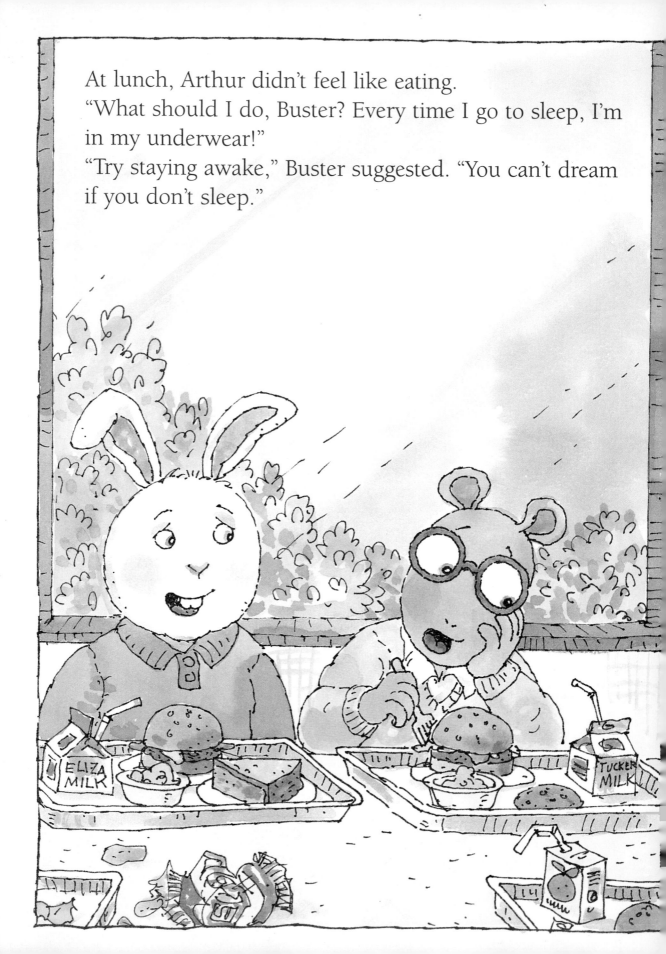

That night, Arthur tried some tricks to stay awake.

Old MacDonald had a farm...

But as hard as he tried,
Arthur just couldn't.

"I'll get you, Verminator.... After ... I take ... a
little nap."

In Arthur's dream, the Verminator was torturing the class by scratching his claws on the blackboard. Hearing cries for help, Bionic Arthur rushed to the rescue!

But as he entered the classroom to take on the Verminator, everyone started laughing.

"My pants!" Arthur gasped as he woke up with a start. "Rise and shine, Mr. Fancy Pants," said D.W. "They're right here. Mom says you better shake a leg or you'll be late for school!"

Arthur asked Buster for some emergency advice on
the way to school.
"It even happens when I'm a superhero!" he exclaimed.
"I can't stay awake forever. I'm doomed!"
"Maybe you should sleep in your pants," said Buster.
"That way you won't have to worry about putting
them on."

That night, D.W. came into Arthur's room.
"Why are you wearing your pants to bed?" she asked.
"Because . . . ah . . . that way I can be ready for school
faster," he said quickly.

"I'm going to ask Mom if I can sleep in my clothes, too,"
D.W. said. "And maybe my coat and boots. *Mom?!*"
Arthur sighed and changed into his pajama pants.

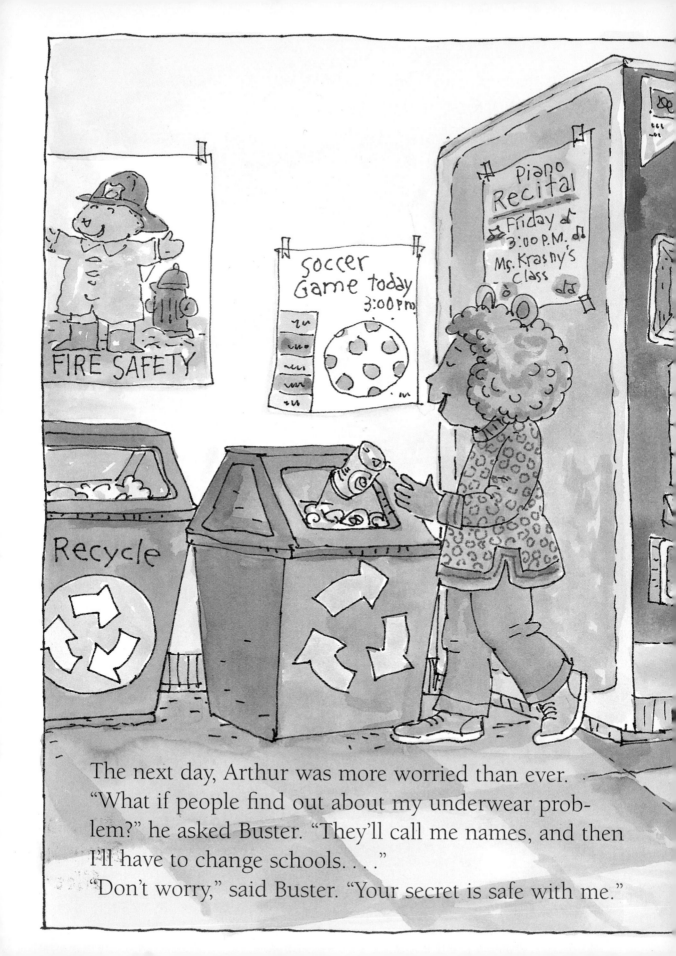

The next day, Arthur was more worried than ever. "What if people find out about my underwear problem?" he asked Buster. "They'll call me names, and then I'll have to change schools. . . ."

"Don't worry," said Buster. "Your secret is safe with me."

At lunch the following day, Arthur sat with Francine and Muffy. They looked at him and started to giggle. "What's so funny?" Arthur asked.
"Do you have your pants on?" asked Francine. "Better make sure!"

Arthur checked. He *was* wearing pants.
He moved to another table.
"I heard about your nightmares," said the Brain, "so I
got out a couple of books on dreams. Apparently, you
have a pathological fear of embarrassment. . . ."

Arthur got up to find Buster.

"Buster!" cried Arthur. "You told everyone about my underwear dreams!"

"Not everyone," replied Buster. "Only a few kids."

"Buster, how could you?"

"Well, I couldn't help you. I needed some advice."

"This is so embarrassing!" said Arthur.

When Arthur turned to run out of the cafeteria,
his pants pocket got caught.

RRRIPPP!

Everyone in the cafeteria began to laugh.
Arthur couldn't move.
But Binky grabbed two trays to cover him.
"Quick!" he whispered. "Into the kitchen!"

Mrs. MacGrady wrapped her apron around Arthur and got out a needle and thread.

"I'm sorry," Buster said. "I shouldn't have told anyone."

"It's okay," said Arthur sadly. "You were just trying to help. The hard part will be telling my parents that I have to change schools."

Mrs. MacGrady handed Arthur his pants.

"Thanks," said Arthur. "Is there a back door?"

"Afraid not," said Mrs. MacGrady. "But do you know the old saying, 'A banana without its peel is still a banana'?"

"Huh?" said Arthur and Buster.

"It means people get embarrassed all the time," Binky explained.

"But you're still Arthur," said Mrs. MacGrady. "A smart, kind young man — with or without your pants."

Arthur smiled.

A few days later, Arthur met Buster at the Sugar Bowl.
"Well, no more underwear nightmares!" Arthur said.
"That's great!" said Buster. "I never thought that ripping
your pants in the cafeteria would be the thing to cure
you."
As they stood up to leave, Arthur looked at Buster and
frowned.
"Uh, Buster . . . I think you forgot something."

Buster woke up with a scream.
"Uh-oh," he sighed. "Here we go again!"